GERTRUDE THE CHUBBY UNICORN

BOOK ONE: GERTRUDE TAKES THE CAKE

JUSTIN JOHNSON

CCS
Publishing

Gertrude
THE CHUBBY
Unicorn

Book One:
Gertrude Takes The Cake

Justin
Johnson

CONTENTS

PROLOGUE: THE WHERE GERTRUDE LIVES CHAPTER

*D*ear Reader,

There is a place in a far off land…a land unlike anything you've ever seen before.

It is a place where all of the creatures of folk lore live; a place where creatures can fly; a place where the rushing rapids taste of raspberry; a place with hotdog hills, cake coves, and even a fancy pants forest where every tree has it's own fashion designer.

This place is called The Island of Fru Fru.

And in this place, there lives a unicorn.

Actually, there are several unicorns who live there… but there is one who is…how do I put this?

Special.

You see, when most of us are asked to picture a

unicorn, we dream up some majestic horselike creatures with a beautiful mane, a long, flowing tail, and a perfect horn.

They have fancy names like Celestia, Mystery, or Aerowynn.

And don't get me wrong, there are some unicorns on The Island of Fru Fru that have names and features like that.

But not the one I'm thinking of.

No.

The unicorn I'm thinking of is a unicorn named Gertrude.

And Gertrude is not like other unicorns in the ways we mentioned above.

You see, Gertrude is...and I'm trying not to hurt anyone's feelings when I say this, but it's simply the truth.

Gertrude, well, she's chubby.

Very round, actually.

Because she likes to eat.

A lot.

And she doesn't get enough exercise, either.

Anyhow, this is her story. And these are her adventures.

I hope you enjoy, Gertrude Takes the Cake.

Happy Reading,

Justin Johnson

The author of this incredibly stupid series about a fat unicorn who finds a way to save the day!

THE PROBLEM AT HAND CHAPTER

*O*ne lovely afternoon on the Island of Fru Fru, a chubby unicorn named Gertrude sat down on her couch to enjoy a large pizza and a 2 liter of cola.

She wished that she could say this was a treat, but this was actually the norm. Well, it was the norm for her.

As she took bite after bite and sip after sip, she stared out the window. She wasn't looking at anything special. She was just staring off. And eating. And eating. And staring off.

The view was spectacular.

Her window opened up to a beautiful rolling field of green. It was the kind of field where wild flowers of all types and colors would pop up and attract butterflies and many other wondrous creatures.

Just past these superb flowers was a massive waterfall.

From where Gertrude sat, she could see both the top and bottom of the fall. It was a sight to behold. Plus, it made the most wonderful sound as the water fell over the edge and down to the pool below.

Gertrude loved that noise.

It had helped her get to sleep for many years now. She would lay down on her bed, nestle her head into her pillow, and listen to the *whoosh, whoosh, whoosh*. She was sure there were more *whooshes* than that, but she never made it to the fourth *whoosh* before she was fast asleep and adding her own noises to the cacophony of nighttime noises that the Island of Fru Fru was famous for.

But she wasn't thinking of any of that. She was only thinking about the taste of the greasy pepperoni. It was fantastic. And when she took a chug of cola — right from the bottle — that sugary elixir melded so well with the salty cheese that Gertrude couldn't think of much in her world that was better.

Just as she was finished chewing her fourth slice, and started to reach for a fifth, her cell phone rang.

Yeah, I know it's weird.

A unicorn.

With a cell phone.

But let me remind you, that you are reading a story about the Island of Fru Fru.

Did you really think it was going to be realistic?

I mean, come on!

Anyway, back to the story.

Where was I?

Oh yeah, Gertrude's cell phone rang just as she was picking up her fifth piece of pizza. That's where I was.

Well, Gertrude took a huffy breath. She wasn't a fan of being interrupted while she was indulging in the finer things life had to offer.

Her phone was on the table next to her. So, it wasn't like she had to actually get up to get it, either.

Even so, she was irritated.

Starlight.

She read her best friend's name from the screen.

What does she want now? Gertrude thought. She would have said it out loud, as she was alone. But she had food in her mouth and wasn't sure that it was all going to stay there. So she just thought about the annoyance her friend's call was causing her.

Starlight was always calling Gertrude for some reason or another. And usually, the reasons were not that important. But there were other times when the reasons were quite important.

One might even say, dire.

And that is not hyperbole. Which is pronounced

JUSTIN JOHNSON

High-per-bo-lee. It means that I'm not exaggerating when I use the word dire.

According to the dictionary, the word dire means: indicating trouble, disaster, misfortune, or the like.

And there were times when this definition applied to one of Starlight's calls.

So, Gertrude had a tough decision to make.

She stared at the fifth slice of pizza she was getting ready to eat.

And then she looked to the phone, which was on its second ring.

Back to the pizza.

Then to the phone.

Ring three.

Pizza.

Phone.

Ring four.

A deep sigh.

And then the sound of Gertrude wiping her hooves clean with a napkin.

She chewed a little faster than was comfortable, hoping that she would have an empty mouth by the time she hit the 'Accept' button on the phone.

Unfortunately, by the time she got to the phone, Starlight had hung up.

Gertrude said, 'huh…'

And then turned back to grab that fifth slice of pizza.

The phone started ringing again.

'Oh, for heaven's sake!' Gertrude bellowed.

She pressed the 'Accept' button and said, "Hello?!" It came out of her mouth in a way that let Starlight know Gertrude was annoyed.

"Did I catch you at a bad time?" Starlight asked.

"You always do," Gertrude snapped, remembering that the last time this happened she was just getting started on her fifth slice of pizza. And the time before that was exactly the same. And come to think of it, the time before the time before that too.

"I sincerely apologize," Starlight continued, "But this is urgent!"

"Urgent?" Gertrude asked. "Or *dire?*"

"What's the difference?" Starlight wondered.

"So urgent means that something has do be done fast. But dire means that the thing that has to be done is going to be super dangerous," Gertrude informed her friend.

"Hmmm..." Starlight thought. "I always thought they meant pretty much the same thing. Well, I would have to say that this one is definitely urgent, and it could also possibly be dire, depending on what we end up finding."

Sweet, thought Gertrude, who was always up for an

adventure even if it interrupted her pizza eating
sessions.

"What's going on, then?" Gertrude inquired.

"The cake for the Island of Fru Fru's 500 millionth
birthday party has disappeared!"

Gertrude couldn't see Starlight, but her voice
certainly seemed dire enough.

"Disappeared, you say? Go on..."

Starlight continued. "I've been working so hard on
this cake, Gertrude. You know how important baking
and birthdays are to me."

Gertrude did, in fact, know how important these
things were to Starlight. At times, Starlight bordered on
obsessive about every last detail for every birthday party
she ever had the privilege of planning. And the cake,
being the pinnacle of the birthday party experience, was
usually the detail that she stressed the most about.

"I do," Gertrude agreed.

"Well, you can imagine how important *this* birthday
party is for me. I mean, how many times does an Island
turn 500 million years old?"

"Once," Gertrude said. "It would turn 500 million
years old exactly one time. Actually, if you wish to get
all philosophical about things, we could say that it
really doesn't matter what you're talking about — an
island, a country, an animal, a human — they only turn
each age one time."

"Are you finished?" Starlight said, sounding annoyed. Gertrude decided to let it go.

"Yes," Gertrude said. "Sorry."

"Apology accepted," Starlight said graciously. "So, as I was saying before, this birthday is a really, really big deal. And I was nominated to be the leader of the Island of Fru Fru's 500 Millionth Birthday Party Leadership Planning Committee. It was a very prestigious honor, one I will be able to tell my grand children about some day. You know what I mean?"

"Yup."

Gertrude's voice had a mild tone of disinterest in it. And though Starlight was getting ready to launch into the entire planning process and all that had led up to this very moment, she thought better of it. She knew that if she didn't cut her story short and get to the point, then she would lose Gertrude's interest.

And if she lost Gertrude's interest, then she'd get no help from her.

And she needed Gertrude's help.

"That's where you come in," Starlight pivoted. "The cake I've been working so hard on has gone missing. And I need you and Nightwatch to come over and help me find it."

Gertrude hung up the phone without saying goodbye.

She took two quick bites of that fifth slice of pizza, and then threw the rest into the box.

It took her two large bounds to get to her front door.

She threw it open and proclaimed:

"This is an adventure for Gertrude the Chubby Unicorn!"

THE TRYING TO FIND THE EASY ANSWER CHAPTER

S tarlight was sitting at her kitchen table when Gertrude knocked on the door.

"Come in," she said.

Gertrude opened the door and announced, "Have no fear, Gertrude the Chubby Unicorn is here!"

Starlight's face puckered. "That doesn't sound very good. I can't tell if it's the use of the word 'chubby', or if you messed up the meter and made the second part of it too long to possibly rhyme 'here' convincingly with the 'fear'."

"Listen," Gertrude said, clearly miffed. "I'm not writing a rhyming children's book or anything. I'm just announcing my presence and the reason for my presence in one quick catch phrase."

"Well, I'd keep working on it," Starlight said. She

moved toward the sink to continue her clean up efforts. "By the way," she said, "You couldn't have said 'good-bye' before you hung up the phone?"

"Sorry about that," Gertrude said, shutting the door behind her and moving over to Starlight. "It's just that sometimes I like to pretend that I'm starring in my own movie and the camera's rolling. Hanging up the phone was just part of increasing the dramatic tension. You get it, right?"

Starlight shook her head.

"That's okay."

Gertrude walked away, not wanting Starlight to see her face, which had drooped considerably. If her friend kept this up, this adventure would be no fun...no fun at all. Certainly not worthy of a movie, and barely worthy of a book.

"So, anyway," Gertrude continued as she sat down at the table, "this cake. When did it go missing?"

"I don't know the exact time," Starlight said. She was cleaning up the counter and putting frosting and sprinkles away. She also had a slew of candles that were in a big box. "Can you help me pick these up?"

Gertrude stood up, and the two unicorns moved the box out of the kitchen and into the dining room. Gertrude was shocked to see that the whole wall of the Starlight's dining room was full of candle boxes.

"How many boxes do you have?"

"Oh, this is nothing," Starlight bragged. "There's at least four times as many boxes in the basement. You know, 500 million years requires 500 million candles — and that takes a lot of boxes of candles."

Gertrude nodded, obviously impressed. Then a thought occurred to her. "So, who's going to blow all the candles out?"

"I'm not totally sure," Starlight said, staring at the boxes upon boxes of candles in front of her. "I didn't actually think about it."

Gertrude noted the look on Starlight's face. Starlight was easily stressed out. And this major detail not being accounted for, would surely be enough to send her over the edge.

"Oh no!" Starlight blurted out. "What are we going to do? I mean, here I was, thinking everything was all set; thinking 'way to go Starlight, you really rocked this', and now it's all falling apart."

Gertrude knew that Starlight's next move would be to flop onto the floor and sulk. And once she hit the floor, there was no way of getting her up again until she was good and ready to get up on her own.

In Gertrude's experience that could be a few hours, or less. But she'd also seen Starlight go weeks without picking herself up.

The key was to keep her in good spirits, so it didn't come to that. And with the Island of Fru Fru's 500 millionth in less than a day, Gertrude had to think fast.

"Hey," Gertrude called out. "Don't worry about the candles...we don't even have a cake to put them on."

This did not have the desired effect on Starlight. She threw her hooves up in the air and covered her head. And then started to fall to the floor when...

CRASH!!

IT SOUNDED like a window breaking in the next room.

This was enough to get Starlight to snap back. She stood up and walked toward the living room.

"Who's there?" she called out.

"It's just me," the familiar and dejected voice of Nightwatch returned.

Gertrude and Starlight walked into the living room to see their friend, Nightwatch, emerging from a pile of broken glass. There was now a gentle breeze coming in from the once closed window. The breeze was cool, and was moving the curtains back and forth in a mesmerizing way.

Starlight, however, was not mesmerized.

"What were you thinking?!?" she scolded.

Nightwatch looked up. He had a purple bandana on

his head, with holes cut out for his horn, eyes and ears. He thought it made him look cool, but if one were to ask Gertrude or Starlight, they'd say it made him look completely foolish.

"I was just trying to get in to the house," he answered, weakly. "Honestly, Starlight, it's not my fault you keep your windows so clean."

Starlight's windows were always kept incredibly clean. In the last three days alone, no fewer than twenty birds had flown into them, thinking that there was nothing there at all. Thankfully, no casualties had occurred.

But backhanded compliment or not, Starlight wasn't going to just let Nightwatch get away with this.

"I don't really see what my clean windows have to do with you acting like a moron." She pointed toward the kitchen. "I mean, I have a door for crying out loud. Would it really be so bad if you just used it every once in a while?"

Nightwatch stood up and started picking shards of glass out of his legs and chest. "Gertrude," he asked, "There are a few pieces of glass near my tail. I can't reach them. Would you be a dear?"

Gertrude tried to bore a hole into Nightwatch's face with her eyes. It didn't work, and she ended up walking around the pile of broken glass, trying her best not to step on any of it. When she got to the backside of

Nightwatch, she made sure that each piece of glass she removed was 'accidentally' pushed in just a little bit before it was pulled out.

Nightwatch returned his attention to Starlight. "You want me to just come through the kitchen door? When I've got this amazing jumping ability?"

"Yes. I do."

"Dude! That's sooooo boring!" Nightwatch retorted.

This was his new catch phrase, and both Gertrude and Starlight found it incredibly immature and obnoxious.

After a small bit of bickering back and forth, and some more painful glass removal, Nightwatch was eventually glass free and swept up the mess he'd made.

The three unicorns then moved back to the kitchen.

Gertrude started opening and closing cupboards. Then she moved to the refrigerator and freezer, and then she opened up the oven and took a peek inside.

"What, may I ask, are you doing?" Starlight said.

"I'm just making sure that the cake isn't still somewhere in here."

"I told you already, it's gone."

"I know," Gertrude said. "And it's not that I don't trust you. It's just, if we're going to go on a new adventure and find this bad boy of a birthday cake, we need to be absolutely sure that it's not here."

"Can I ask you a question?" Starlight asked.

"You just did," Nightwatch chuckled.

Starlight shot him a glance that made him stop laughing at his own joke.

"Why are you always trying to find the easy answer?"

"I will answer your question, with a question," Gertrude said. "Why aren't you? I mean, think about it. If we can do something the easy way, shouldn't we? Really? Does everything have to be difficult?"

Starlight thought about this for a minute. "No," she finally said. "It doesn't have to be difficult. But I already told you that the cake is missing, didn't I?"

"Sure," Gertrude said. "I was just double checking."

"I think I know where the cake is," Nightwatch chimed in. He sat down at the kitchen table and invited Starlight and Gertrude to join him.

They sat down.

"So, you're not going to like this — especially you, Gertrude."

"Why not?" Gertrude asked.

"We're going to have to fly...for a long time," Nightwatch said. "I don't want to hurt your feelings, but you know you're not exactly in flying shape."

"What's that supposed mean?" Gertrude said, indignantly. But deep down she knew that Nightwatch was telling her the truth.

"It's just the truth," he said. "And this is also just

the truth — the cake you baked, Starlight...it's been taken to Captured Cake Cove."

"You don't mean..." Starlight said.

Nightwatch nodded. "I do."

The name came from the three unicorns in unison, for now they knew who was responsible for the disappearance of the Island of Fru Fru's 500 millionth birthday cake.

"Cray Cray."

THE TIME TO RIDE CHAPTER

C ray Cray was Captured Cake Cove's Crazy Kooky King and Captain of The Cake Capturers.

He oversaw the entire cake capturing operation.

And he had set to work to foil Starlight's plans to celebrate the Island of Fru Fru's 500 millionth birthday celebration.

The only question was…

"Why?" Starlight asked. "Doesn't he have enough cakes already. I mean, you've seen the Cove, right? It's a travesty what all those cakes are doing to the sea life, isn't it?"

Nightwatch and Gertrude were caught off guard by this last little outburst. They both figured that Starlight would stick to her own, selfish, questions regarding the disappearance of her cake. They never would have guessed that she would go all environmentalist on the whole situation.

"Well," Nightwatch began tentatively. "I don't know much about the effects the cakes are having on the wild life in the area, but I think I might know why Cray Cray has set out to spoil the Island's birthday."

"And why's that?" Starlight asked.

"It's really pretty simple."

"Enlighten us."

"Are you ready for it?"

Starlight stood up from the table and raised her front hoof. "Are *you* ready for it?"

"He hates us," Nightwatch said, wincing and covering his head, for fear that he might end up with a horseshoe shaped bruise. "That's it. He just hates us. All of us that inhabit the inland of the island."

"You really think it's that simple?" Gertrude piped up.

"I do," said Nightwatch.

Starlight put her hoof back on the floor with the others.

"Alright," she said. "I guess there's only one thing to do — we have to go to Captured Cake Cove and see if there's any real truth to your theory."

The three unicorns left Starlight's house and got a

running start. Within a few steps all three of them were magically floating and flying overhead.

Starlight, as she was the most eager to see if this was going to pan out, was in the lead. And it wasn't even close. She was way ahead of the other two. But eventually, she would slow down. Pacing is very important when traveling long distances.

Nightwatch was in the middle. He was paced perfectly and had not a care in the world, nor a worry that Starlight would eventually settle in and fly right. However, he was quiet concerned about…

Gertrude was sucking wind — already. They had just left the ground thirty seconds earlier and she was already struggling to keep up. Forget about pacing with her, it would be a miracle if she was just able to cross the finish line, so to speak.

"You okay?" Nightwatch called back.

"Don't talk to me," Gertrude snapped between deep breaths.

"Okay," Nightwatch said, not really knowing when to stop. "It's just that…I mean…it doesn't look like you're going to make it, is all."

"If you don't shut it, you're not going to make it." Gertrude called out. It sounded like she was going to vomit. The words came out sounding forced and guttural.

"You'd have to catch me first!" Nightwatch teased.

And then he turned on the burners and caught up to Starlight.

Go ahead, just keep it up Nightwatch. I know where you live. I'll punch you in your sleep, Gertrude *thought,* because by now she had developed so much metallic tasting saliva in her mouth, she was afraid to open it for fear that she would end up leaving an unwanted gift on the homes below.

Meanwhile, up ahead, Nightwatch had caught up to Starlight.

"Do you have a plan for this?" he asked.

"No," Starlight said.

"Just gonna wing it...that's a good idea."

Starlight did not appreciate the joke. "I'm going to get answers first and then we'll figure out what to do."

"Oh," said Nightwatch, "I get it! We're going to negotiate and try to get the cake back peacefully...I'm sure that will work with someone as rational and level headed as Cray Cray."

"Do you have a better idea?" Starlight snapped.

"Better than negotiating with a crazy person... hmmm, let me think — yup!"

Again, Starlight did not appreciate the sarcasm and insults Nightwatch was whipping up today. He was in one of his moods. Normally, she could weather the storm, but the situation today required her to have super unicorn coping skills, which, sadly, she did not.

"If you don't start speaking more directly, you're not going to get any of the cake when we finally do find it," Starlight threatened.

"Oooh, is that a birthday cake threat?"

"It is," Starlight smiled. She hated that she couldn't stay mad at Nightwatch. He was a big jerk. But he was their jerk — and she loved him for it.

"Anyway, what would your plan of action be?"

"Well," Nightwatch began, "I would most definitely land all stealth and ninja like. I'd make sure that I wasn't seen and then I'd go searching for your cake — completely undetected — did I mention that already?"

"Yeah," Starlight said. "You did."

"Alright. 'Cause it's like wicked important. If we're seen or heard this plan becomes no bueno, and then we have to resort to your plan. And that would probably be a big flop too. Because if life has taught me one thing it's that negotiating with an angry crazy person is the only thing more difficult than negotiating with a happy crazy person."

"So, that's it? We sneak around the Cove and try to find our cake before the Cake Captors and Cray Cray find us? That sounds just as weak as mine!"

Starlight flew for a minute with this thought rattling around in her head. And then she asked, "I wonder if Gertrude has some better ideas?"

Gertrude was actually falling farther and farther

behind with each passing second. She has passed Sugar Cookie Mountain, and it made her want to stop and eat.

And then she passed the Goodie Goodie Gumdrop Forest, and she wanted to stop and have a treat.

And then there was the icing on the cake, so to speak. The Rushing Raspberry Rapids were just below her, and it was all she could do to stay airborne and not dive right in to get herself a drink.

But she knew that her friends needed her, and she wasn't about to let them down.

Captured Cake Cove was just at the end of the Rushing Raspberry Rapids. And as she reached the end of them, dreams of Raspberry Punch rushing past her lips, she felt herself getting heavier.

It felt like a rock was in her stomach pulling her downward toward the rapids. She fought against the sudden force, but it was no use. She was going down, and she was going down fast.

How could I have been so stupid? She found herself thinking. *If only I'd eaten less pizza, and less...everything. Then this wouldn't be happening, would it?*

"Help!" she called out. "Please...Starlight! Night-watch! Help!"

But it was no use. No one was going to come rescue old chubby Gertrude.

Not this time.

She would surely fall into the Raspberry Rapids with a plunk, and be taken away with the sweet taste of fruit juice, never to be seen or heard from again.

Where were they? She thought. *Where were her most precious friends now, in the hour of her need? Had they even noticed that she was gone? Had they noticed that she'd fallen behind so far that there was no way she would ever catch —*

That thought was interrupted by something.

You see, as Gertrude continued her slow and steady plummet toward the rushing juice below, she saw two dots in the distance.

At first, they didn't look like anything—a few birds, perhaps. But as she investigated further and squinted her eyes to try and see what they were, it became apparent that she wasn't falling because she was fat after all!

A great sense of relief came over Gertrude as she saw Starlight and Nightwatch plummeting as well.

Ha! It wasn't just me being fat!

And then, as quickly as this good feeling had arrived, it flew away.

Gertrude suddenly realized that if she was falling… and her friends were falling…then none of them were going to make it to Captured Cake Cove.

And if they did, it was going to be covered in sticky juice from the Raspberry Rapids.

That was the last thought she remembered thinking before the sweet smell of raspberry rushed right up her nose...and Gertrude began to sink.

THE INTRODUCTION OF THE BADDY CHAPTER

*G*ertrude was being tossed about like a kite in the wind. She had no control over her own body.

What was worse, was that she was completely unable to see Starlight or Nightwatch anywhere.

For all she knew, they had been completely taken under by the current.

She couldn't waste her thoughts on them at this moment, though. She had to worry about her own survival.

Her speed was increasing and every time she went under, it seemed longer than the time before. Gertrude wasn't sure if she was just out of breath and getting tired of fighting the rapids, or if the rapids were pulling her down deeper and harder than they had before.

"Grab on!" she heard Nightwatch's familiar voice.

Gertrude tried to open her eyes and locate whatever it was that she was supposed to grab hold of, and then she was pulled down again.

"Come on, Gertrude!" This time it was Starlight's voice. "It's no use," she heard her friend say. "She can't see it!"

"Hold on," Nightwatch said to her.

And then Gertrude felt something around her neck. And then there was a tug and she was drifting to her right. The current that had been to her back was now rushing up against her chest and the front of her neck as she was quickly spun around.

The pressure that had been at the front of her throat was now position on the back of her neck. She could feel it digging in hard, but she knew that if she could just withstand it for a few more moments then she would be safely on land with her friends.

"Good job, Nightwatch!" Starlight was yelling.

"I'm not there yet. Don't start celebrating until we've got her up here with us," he said cautiously.

Within five seconds of Nightwatch saying this, Gertrude felt something hit her front hooves...and then her back hooves.

She tumbled and fell sideways, and the pressure from whatever was around her neck had completely stopped.

"It's shallow enough that you can stand up now," Starlight told her.

Nightwatched walked over and began to take the rope off of Gertrude's neck, slipping it over her head carefully.

"That was close," said Gertrude as she stood up. It was difficult to find her footing and she was breathing heavily from the whole ordeal.

"Watch your step," Starlight warned. "It's pretty slippery until we get up to the mainland."

Gertrude's eyes made their way to where Nightwatch was now walking.

She'd never been to Captured Cake Cove before.

She'd never had a reason.

But she'd heard all about it. And now that she was here in unicorn for the first time, she was complete amazed.

Never in her life had she seen so many cakes.

There was every kind of cake you could ever dream of, just strewn about the shore line, and deep into the mainland. The trees and rocks were adorned with cakes as well.

Birthday cakes, wedding cakes, Bar Mitzva cakes, baby shower cakes, retirement party cakes — all of them were here.

"So this is captured cake cove!" Gertrude exclaimed.

"SHHHH!" Nightwatch shushed her, bringing his

hoof up to his mouth. He continued in a whisper. "You weren't there for the discussion that Starlight and I had. But we are going to try to find this cake ninja style — without a trace. Which means no talking, or exclaiming, or shouting, or any of that stuff that you might find yourself wanting to do right now. I get that this place must be pretty cool for you and all, but let's keep focused on the task at hand."

"What's that supposed to mean?" Gertrude said, clearly upset with Nightwatch, and clearly disregarding the plan he'd just set forth.

"Nothing," Nightwatch fired back. "It's just—"

All of the sudden, as if out of nowhere, our heroes heard the most maniacal of all the maniacal laughs in whole wide world of worlds.

And they knew exactly who it belonged to.

"Ha, ha, ha, ha, ha!"

They knew that laugh, though they'd never met the man at the other end of it.

Cray Cray's laugh came from behind a series of wedding cakes. They could hear it loud and clear, but they couldn't see him...yet.

Finally, he stepped out from behind a six foot tall, five layer wedding cake. He was wearing a white tuxedo. The top three buttons of his shirt were undone and his black bow tie was dangling over his shoulders.

A smear of light blue frosting was smeared on his left lapel.

"Well, well, well," he said, bringing his hands together in front of his face. This was also covered in frosting. His black hair was slicked back and greasy, and his two beady eyes peek out from behind dirty glasses.

"I thought you'd never show up," he continued when he was finished swallowing the bite of cake he had in his mouth. "Better late than never, that's what I always say!"

"Oh," Gertrude said, "Is that what you always say?"

"As a matter of fact...no!" Cray Cray said. "I've never said it before in my life. You win. You're too good for me. I'm no match for you and your super unicorn sleuths. You may take your cake and go back to your regularly scheduled slate of events."

"Really," Starlight said, stepping forward.

Cray Cray smiled. "No! Of course not. However, I would like to take the opportunity to welcome you all to Captured Cake Cove."

He moved back behind the wedding cake and took a swipe of frosting with his hand.

"You should make yourselves at home," he said, putting the frosting up to his lips. "I think you're going to be here a very long time."

THE REASON THE BADDY DID THAT
THING CHAPTER

*G*ertrude could feel her mouth begin to water. And it had nothing to do with the Raspberry Rapids.

It had to do with the mountain of cake surrounding her. She was in chubby unicorn heaven. This thought almost made her forget about the situation at hand.

But then she got even more excited, because this situation was now in the process of becoming extremely dire.

And dire's what she loved about adventuring.

"Just give us the cake," Starlight stepped forward. "We already know you have it."

Cray Cray clapped his hands together. Frosting splattered everywhere. "Very good, young unicorn. I'm sorry, but I didn't catch your name."

"Starlight."

"That truly is a beautiful name," Cray Cray said. "Now, if you'll excuse me for a moment, I just got frosting all over myself and a change of clothes is necessary before we continue."

He reached out his left hand and pulled out a rolling rack from behind another tall wedding cake.

The rack was full of clothing of all sorts. Most of the outfits were covered in frosting and cake crumbs.

"You'd think with all of these cakes, and so little clothing, that I would have found a worthy dry cleaner by now. Alas, I don't leave the Cove much."

He moved his frosting covered fingers from one outfit to the next, commenting on each one.

"Should I wear a birthday outfit?" he asked, putting his finger on what looked to be a clown costume.

"Or, maybe...just maybe, a Christening suit." The suit was dark blue, with a shirt and a neck tie.

"Oooh," Cray Cray exclaimed, moving on to the next outfit. "Ugly sweaters are all the rage, aren't they? I know it's a little warm today, but Christmas is such fun season, isn't it?"

And then, as quickly as he'd brought the rack out, he proclaimed, "Blah. Nothing fits me anyway. All this cake is making me fat!" And he pushed the rack back behind the cake.

"This old wedding tux will have to do for today, I suppose."

The three unicorns look on, not really knowing what to do. Nightwatch was right about one thing: Cray Cray was cray cray.

"So, why did you do it?" Starlight finally asked.

"Do what?" Cray Cray replied, playing coy. This dude was off his rocker, and getting a clear answer from him was going to be beyond difficult.

"Why did you take my cake?"

"Oh, was that your cake?" Cray Cray asked. "I was under the impression that it belonged to the Island of Fru Fru. Do you think that the island officials would love to hear their beloved...Starlight, did you say?"

Starlight stood still, refusing to answer.

"Yes," Cray Cray laughed. "Starlight. So, how do you think the island officials would react to the news that their lovely Starlight was claiming ownership over something that was clearly meant to be shared with everyone? Do you think they'd like that?"

"You know what I meant," Starlight shot back. "Why did you take the cake?"

"I'm sorry," Cray Cray said. He turned and motioned to the thousands of cakes surrounding him. "You'll have to be a tad more specific. I have a lot of cakes here. I don't know if you noticed." He winked at Starlight.

This sent her over the edge and she started to charge.

Nightwatch ran in front of her and cut her off. He looked at her tensely. "Don't do this," he said quietly. "Just stay calm. We'll figure this out."

"Oh, that's good," Cray Cray chortled. "'We'll figure this out'," he mocked Nightwatch.

Nightwatch turned toward Cray Cray and looked as though he was about to charge when Cray Cray finally told them what they'd been wondering.

"So, you want to know why I took the cake, huh? Well, let me tell you."

He walked over to the wedding cake he'd been eating when they'd arrived and sat down on the bottom layer.

The sound of squishing cake made Gertrude wince. *What a waste,* she thought.

"500 million years," Cray Cray began. "That's a lot of years, no?"

Starlight nodded her head.

"And what has that stupid island done in those 500 million years?"

Cray Cray sat forward, the cake squishing again, and hunks of frosting and cake falling off the front of it.

"Nothing! The Island of Fru Fru has done absolutely NOTHING! Now, I ask you, if someone does nothing, should they get something? I say, no. They shouldn't get anything, let alone a huge birthday bash with a magical birthday cake!"

"Magical?" Nightwatch asked. "What do you mean magic?"

"Why don't you go ahead and ask your friend, Starlight, what I mean? She'll tell you all about it!"

Nightwatch and Gertrude focused in on Starlight.

Starlight swallowed hard and said, "It's impossible to make a single cake big enough to feed an entire island. So, I had to impart some magic into the cake batter. The cake I made regenerates. Every time a slice is cut and removed from the cake, that slice grows back. That way everyone will get a piece."

"That sounds amazing!" Gertrude exclaimed.

"Yeah," agreed Nightwatch. "I agree. Very cool!"

"The problem is," Starlight continued, "to make a cake like that takes months, and now that that creep over there has stolen it, there's no time to make another one — we have to find the one I made!"

"Creep..." Cray Cray said. "That's very original. I've never heard that before."

"Well, it's true," Starlight said. "I mean, who steals a birthday cake? You'd have to be a creep to want to ruin the celebration for everyone else."

"Well listen, I'm not that bad," he said. And then he looked around as if to make sure no one would hear what he was about to say. "If I was that bad, would I give you an opportunity to find your cake? Well, that's exactly what I'm going to do. I'm going to give you the once in a lifetime chance to find your exact cake — not a look a like, not a replica...yours!"

Starlight was less than impressed by this offer. In fact she was pretty darn mad about the whole thing.

"Great," she grumped. "Just tell us what we have to do and kindly move out of the way so we can."

"Oooh! She's chomping at the bit to get started." Cray Cray rubbed his hands together. "I love it!"

He stood up, somehow ignoring the cake that was stuck on the back of his tuxedo, and walked over to a gigantic mountain of cakes.

They were all chocolate, and all about the same size as Starlight's magic 500 millionth birthday cake.

"Do you see these cakes?" he asked.

The three unicorns nodded as one.

"Your cake is in there somewhere. But, you see, all of the cakes look pretty much the same. And they all taste pretty much the same, too. But only one of them is magic. That one's yours."

"And you're just going to let us get in there and take it if we can find it?" Starlight asked.

"Pretty much," Cray Cray shrugged.

Gertrude stepped up next to Starlight.

"Let's do this!"

THE 'OH NO YOU DIDN'T' CHAPTER

*G*ertrude stepped up to the mountain of cakes first. She examined each cake as best she could, but she could find no difference from cake to cake.

They all looked so similar.

"This is going to be impossible," she said.

"We've gotta do something," said Nightwatch. "We can't just let this bozo win. Starlight, is there anything that would help us identify your cake as different somehow?"

"Come to think of it, there might be," Starlight said, stepping forward. "I had to use so much magic on it that the frosting pattern differs significantly from most of the cakes we're looking at now. Do you see the slight ridges along the sides of these cakes?"

Nightwatch and Gertrude took close looks at the cakes. And then they looked at each other. Both of them had something in their eyes, and they recognized it in the other one as fear. They had no idea what Starlight was talking about.

"Honestly," Gertrude said, figuring she would be the brave one, "I can't see anything. They all look the same to me."

"No, you're absolutely right, Gertrude," Starlight agreed. "But do you see the small ridges that the frosting is making around the edges. It's clear to me that this frosting was applied with a spatula. My cake doesn't have these because I applied the icing using magic."

"So we just have to find the one that looks different?" Nightwatch nodded. "That doesn't sound so hard."

Cray Cray chuckled behind them. "Good luck with that," he teased. "Go ahead, take a good look and see if you can find yours."

"Ignore him," Starlight ordered. "If we're going to do this, we're going to have block him right out."

The three looked at the mountain of cakes, moving their eyes from cake to cake to cake, looking for any frosting differences they could.

After about ten minutes, Gertrude and Nightwatch

both complained that their eyes were watering and they couldn't look at another cake.

"Really?" said Starlight, both surprised and disappointed. "Well, if you're not going to help me look, how are we ever going to find this cake?"

"You mentioned something about regenerating slices earlier," Nightwatch remembered. "Do you think it would work if it was a bite, and not a slice?"

"What are you thinking?" Starlight asked, somewhat excited.

"Well, I'm thinking, if we took one bite out of each cake and the bite didn't grow back, we'd know it wasn't yours. If, however, we bite into your cake, that bite should regenerate and grow back right?"

Starlight smiled and nodded. "That's a brilliant idea!"

"Thanks," Nightwatch beamed. "So, who's going to —" Nightwatch stopped short, suddenly realizing something wasn't right. "Have you seen Gertrude?"

Starlight looked around frantically from side to side, trying to sneak a peak at Gertrude. And then she called out to her.

Starlight and Nightwatch were shocked as Gertrude emerged from the mountain of cakes with chocolate frosting all over every part of her body.

"What?" she asked through a mouthful of cake.

"Nothing," Nightwatch said. "We were just wondering where you went, that's all."

"I was just doing what you said. No sense in wasting time, right?" Gertrude smiled. There was frosting caked onto her teeth and smeared across her lips. She looked a mess.

But a very kind and helpful mess.

"Let me back at it," she said. "Not a minute to spare, you know!"

And with that Gertrude dove back into the massive pile of cakes that were left.

Starlight and Nightwatch decided not to dive in. For one, it was looking crowded in there, and who knew where Gertrude was going to put her teeth once she was surrounded by all those cakes. There's no telling how dangerous such a place could be.

Several minutes later, Gertrude came out carrying the cake they were looking for.

"Here it is!" She proclaimed, holding it high above her head.

"You're sure?" Nightwatch asked.

"Yes, I'm sure."

"Positive?" he asked.

Gertrude shot him a look.

"If we're going to head back with this cake, we need to make sure it's the right one. That's all."

Gertrude took a bite in front of Nightwatch and Starlight. And the cake grew back where Gertrude's teethmarks had been.

But that wasn't enough for Gertrude. She was so put off by her friend questioning her ability to find the correct cake, that she continued to take bites.

One bite after another, after another, after another. Each bite growing back faster than the one before it.

"Does that make you happy?" Gertrude snapped and then took another bite. "Huh?" And then she dug in again. "Do you see this?" And then another bite. "See the cake comes back?" And then she bit again. "Are you happy now?"

"Gertrude," Starlight interrupted. "Honey, you did a great job. I don't want to be rude and sound as though I don't appreciate everything you've done for me and the Island of Fru Fru...but we really should be going now."

Gertrude took one last bite. She looked up and with her mouth full uttered the words, "Oh, boy."

Starlight and Nightwatch turned around to see what Gertrude had seen.

As it turned out, Cray Cray was only partially true to his word.

Yes, it was true that he allowed them to *find* their cake.

However, he, along with his assembled army of

Crazy Cake Capturers that were now surrounding the unicorns, made it more than clear that he had no intention of letting them *leave* with the cake.

THE ESCAPE FROM THE BADDY CHAPTER

The Crazy Cake Capturers surrounded Starlight, Nightwatch and Gertrude.

Gertrude was still chewing her last bite of cake and trying to swallow it as fast as she could.

Her lips were smacking together and she was making quite a bit of noise.

This noise, and the annoyance of the situation, prompted Nightwatch to take note.

"You know, Gertrude," he said over his shoulder, "I can't help but think that if you'd only eaten just a little bit less we might've gotten out of here before all this transpired."

Gertrude was still trying to choke down cake. But it didn't stop her from arguing.

"Are you for real right now?" she barked.

"Yes, I am." Nightwatched turned to look at his friend. She was covered in cake and tears were forming in her eyes. "I'm not trying to be rude. But it's undeniable that just a couple fewer bites would have allowed us to get out of here before they showed up!"

"Oh," Gertrude said. "*Undeniable* you say? Well, here are a few things that I think are *undeniable*, as you so eloquently put it. Do you realize that we wouldn't even have the cake if it wasn't for my eating? You and Starlight just stood there. I was the one who went in and got the cake." She stopped and looked in the direction of Cray Cray and his cronies. "And as far as they're concerned, they were always going to be here to stop us, no matter when we found the cake. And that's simply *undeniable*."

Cray Cray started clapping.

"Very good....Gertrude, is it? You two should really listen to your friend — she's got it figured out." Cray Cray stepped forward and smiled an evil grin. "You see, you were never getting out of here with that cake. And you were foolish to think that I would do something so cray cray. Although if one were to talk about this later, they might say that what I'm doing is very 'cray cray'. Do you see what I did there? I used my name as an adjective to describe the ridiculousness of the moment...but then I tied it back to my name and made the whole thing kind of iconic."

Nobody laughed.

"Tough room," Cray Cray said, tugging on the collar of his tux. "Honestly, I get no respect! Alright, I'm bored. Enough of this waiting around."

He turned to his assembled goons and yelled, "Charge!"

The Crazy Cake Capturers began moving in on the unicorns.

"We have to do something," Starlight shouted.

"Well, what do you think that might be?" Nightwatch asked. "We can't fly, remember. There's like a spell, or something, over this part of the island."

"What about running?"

"Where? Deeper into Cake Cove. We're better off out here fighting these guys ninja style!" Nightwatch snapped himself up onto his hind legs and put his front hooves out in front of himself in fighting position.

While Starlight and Nightwatch were discussing possible escape solutions, Gertrude started to feel something.

It started in her stomach.

And then it moved lower.

It was uncomfortable.

It continued to move, even lower.

And then it seemed to make a turn and headed out.

Pffftttt

"Gertrude! You're a genius," Nightwatch exclaimed.

He hopped up onto a rainbow cloud that looked to be made of cotton candy.

It floated...higher and higher into the air.

And once he got high enough, the breezed took him out the Raspberry Rapids, where he was able to jump off and start flying toward home.

Of course, Nightwatch wouldn't actually fly toward home without his friends. He waited for them.

"Can you do that again?" Starlight asked.

"You bet!" said Gertrude.

Pfffftttt

Another little rainbow colored cotton candy fart cloud emerged. Starlight put the cake on top of this one, and watched as it floated up into the air and was blown to safety toward Nightwatch.

Pfffftttt

This time, Starlight jumped up and caught her ride.

There was just one last cloud to produce, but Gertrude was running out of gas. Thankfully, she caught a wave of anxiety induced adrenaline. This resulted in a quick burst of gas, which was mixed with something else.

A rainbow colored cotton candy fart cloud appeared and Gertrude jumped up onto it.

As she was jumping up onto the cloud, Cray Cray's Crazy Cake Capturers made one last attempt to grab Gertrude.

She let out one last squeeze, which resulted not in a cloud, but in a full fledged sherbet flop.

"Ewwww, gross!" one of the Capturers cried out.

"That's disgusting!" said another.

"What in the what?"

"I don't get paid enough for this!"

And cries like these continued as Gertrude flew to safety.

She'd done it!

As she floated out to her friends, she could hear Cray Cray's laughs turn to cries, and then he threatened, "You'll be sorry!"

But Gertrude had seen enough movies to know that that's never the case.

Starlight and Nightwatch were already flying when Gertrude got to them.

"Great job!" Starlight said.

"Yeah," Nightwatch nodded. "You were amazing!"

"Thank you," said Gertrude, who was still floating on her cloud, though, surely she was past the point where she could have flown on her own.

"Come on," Nightwatch said. "Why don't you hop off your cloud. We'll get home a lot faster."

"You two go on without me," Gertrude said.

"No," Starlight said. "You need to be there with us when we deliver the cake."

"I'm good."

Starlight and Nightwatch looked at each other and shrugged.

"Suit yourself," Nightwatch said.

"Are you sure?" Starlight asked.

"I've never been more sure about anything," Gertrude smiled.

"Okay," Starlight said, and she turned to make her flight back to the center of the Island of Fru Fru.

"I'll see you at the party," Nightwatch said, and he then he turned and flew away, too.

Gertrude was happy to be floating on her cloud, being nudged by the gentle breeze.

Truth be told, she'd eaten so much cake, and had flown so much today already, there was no way she would have made it back.

She was happy to take her sweet little time, while her friends rushed the cake back to its rightful place at the center of the Island of Fru Fru.

THE HAPPY CHAPTER

*E*veryone was there.

If you'd asked Starlight, there had to have been millions, but Nightwatch would have said that it was actually much closer to six or seven hundred thousand.

Whatever the real number was wasn't important. What was important was that the cake was there for the 500 millionth birthday celebration of the Island of Fru Fru, and many of the island's inhabitants had come out to enjoy the festivities.

Starlight stood in the middle of it, looking around in awe.

"I can't believe we did it!" she said to Nightwatch, who was looking around at the impressive spectacle himself.

"I know. It was pretty amazing."

The mayor of the Island of Fru Fru, who was a Pega-corn— which is really just a unicorn with wings — strolled over to Starlight. "I've gotta hand it to you, Starlight, you've really outdone yourself this time."

"Thank you, sir," Starlight beamed with pride. "It was an honor. But I have to tell you, this wouldn't have been possible without Gertrude."

"Gertrude?" the Pegacorn stopped and thought for a moment. "Gertrude...Gertrude...is she that heavy set unicorn I sometimes see you prancing about with?"

"That's her," Starlight said. "But she prefers 'chubby', not heavyset."

"Interesting," the Mayor replied. "So, how does she fit into the planning of this whole thing?"

"Well, it's a long story. Far too long to get into here. Let's just say that she really saved the day."

"Very well then," the Mayor said. "I have to go now and hob nob with some others. It's bad form if the Mayor stands in one spot too long, you know. Some creatures might think that I'm showing favoritism." He winked and then bowed and then turned to do his due diligence in the social realm of acceptable society.

"I heard you mention Gertrude," Nightwatch said, walking over to Starlight. "Not that I was listening in on your conversation, or anything like that." He blushed a little.

"Yeah," Starlight said. "I just told him that Gertrude saved the day. I didn't really go into much detail — I'll do that later, I'm sure. The way this is going, I'll be a shoe in to win the Event Coordinator position for the Island of Fru Fru's Annual Hot Dog Eating Contest in a few months!"

Nightwatched agreed. "You bet. And the way Gertrude ate today, she'll be the odds on favorite to win!"

The two shared a laugh, and then the Mayor stepped up to the podium that was set up in the middle of everything.

"Hello and happy birthday fellow Fru Fruians!"

Everyone cheered. The sound was deafening.

"As you know, this birthday is a very big one. Very big, indeed. It's not every year an island claims its 500 millionth year of existence. I don't think any of us were around when the Island of Fru Fru came to be. But if I had to wager, I'd bet Bob — our resident tortoise — probably came along not too far after..."

The crowd laughed, and a slow, drawl of a voice shouted, "You know it, Mr. Mayor!"

"There's Bob now!" the Mayor exclaimed. "Hey, Bob, give the good folks here a wave, would you?"

Bob raised one arm to wave and promptly fell over onto his side. The crowd cheered, and a few fairies who'd been hovering above Bob swooped down to pick him up.

Bob's face turned red, and he smiled.

And then the Mayor continued.

"In all seriousness," he said, "None of this would have been possible without the help of one very dedicated unicorn. Starlight, why don't you come up here and take a bow."

Starlight, was caught off guard, but wobbled her way through the crowd, trying not to trip and fall as she made her way up front.

When she got there the mayor stood on his hind legs and used his front hooves to start a round of applause for her.

After a few moments of very heavy and appreciative applause, he dropped back down and addressed the crowd again.

"She planned and organized this whole event and even made the cake we're about to eat! And she claims she couldn't have done it without Gertrude! Is Gertrude here? Let's give her a big round of applause as well!"

The crowd cheered, everyone straining their necks to catch a glimpse of Gertrude as she moved through the crowd.

"Where is she?"

"Who's Gertrude?"

"Do you see anything?"

It seemed that Gertrude was nowhere to be found.

"Well," the Mayor said after a few tense moments. "It appears as though Gertrude is not here at the moment...who want's cake?"

The crowd erupted and lined up as Starlight's cake was wheeled out. Three gnomes, each carrying serving knives, followed the cart and began cutting slices. Each slice was regenerated and everyone was pleased.

"That's amazing!" they said.

"Did you see that?"

"Can we have two slices?"

Starlight, satisfied that her cake was a great success, turned to Nightwatch. "Do you think Gertrude made it back?"

"I don't know," Nightwatch said. "I would have thought that she'd have been here for this. We should go check on her."

The two took off toward Gertrude's house.

They knocked on the door.

There was no answer.

They called through the windows.

There was no answer.

Nightwatch jumped through an open window and then went around to open the front door for Starlight.

"Honestly," Starlight rolled her eyes. "You're impossible."

Nightwatch smiled. "I know."

They made their way through Gertrude's house, looking for her and keeping their eyes peeled for any sign that she'd made it home when —

Snoring.

"Did you hear that?" Starlight asked.

Nightwatch nodded and they headed for Gertrude's bedroom.

It was there that they found her, curled up in bed, sleeping soundly.

She was still covered in frosting. It was clear that after all she'd been through, that she had no need for birthday cake!

READ MORE GERTRUDE!!!!

*W*ell, there you have it!

Gertrude saved the day!

And everyone on the Island of Fru Fru was able to celebrate and enjoy the wonderful cake that Starlight made!

Well, everyone except Cray Cray...

Now, did you know that Gertrude's adventures don't stop there?

No, they don't!

In fact, in Gertrude's second adventure, *Gertrude Eats A Dog,* she and her friends find themselves in quite the bind. The Annual Hot Dog Eating Contest is in danger of being cancelled when the hot dog supply goes missing.

But who could be at the bottom of it?

If you're reading the ebook — Click on the image below to read Gertrude's latest adventure...it might just be her biggest adventure yet!

If you're reading the paperback, you can find more Gertrude where you found this book!

REVIEW

*D*ear reader,

I hope you've enjoyed this story. Honestly, it's one of my absolute favorites — but I'm the author, so I'm probably a little bit biased.

I'm hoping if you enjoyed it, that you'd be willing to leave a review for it wherever you bought it.

Reviews are very helpful in letting other readers know if they will enjoy a book, or not.

Thank you very much in advance for your time and effort.

Tootles,

Justin Johnson

You Might Also Enjoy!

42000158R00043

Made in the USA
Columbia, SC
15 December 2018